Hi and Lois ®

BY MORT WALKER
and DIK BROWNE

SLEEPBUSTERS!

TOR

A TOM DOHERTY ASSOCIATES BOOK

HI AND LOIS: SPEEPBUSTERS!

Copyright © 1983 by King Features Syndicate, Inc.

First printing: December 1987

A TOR Book

Published by Tom Doherty Associates, Inc.
49 West 24 Street
New York, N.Y. 10010

ISBN: 0-812-56917-2
CAN. NO.: 0-812-56918-0

Printed in the United States of America

0 9 8 7 6 5 4 3 2 1

THE OLD INDIAN TRAIL

MUSEUM OF POP CULTURE

ZOOLOGICAL DISPLAYS

A CHANGE OF SCENERY

DIK BROWNE

IN THAT CASE, HERE'S A REGIONAL FOOD FAVORITE

8-11

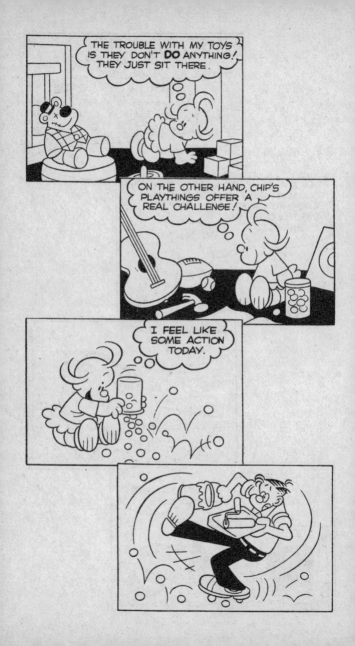

WAIT! DON'T GO!

I'M BUSY, DITTO.

DIK BROWNE

3-20

DAD! I GOT IT NOW! DAD!...

IN SPORTS, TIMING IS EVERYTHING — EVEN FOR THE FANS!